Tales from the Canyons of the Damned

Daniel Arthur Smith

Tales from the Canyons of the Damned No. 20

First Edition

Special thanks to Jessica West

ISBN-13: 978-1946777454 ISBN-10: 1946777455

Cover By Daniel Arthur Smith

Horror Fiction from Holt Smith ltd
Agroland
Tower

~*~

For Susan, Tristan, & Oliver, as all things are.

~*~

The 2K
Eamon Ambrose

~*~

I

"I CAN'T BELIEVE it's almost here."

Henry couldn't sleep. The culmination of ten years of hard work and collaboration was about to come to fruition. A new era, not just for mankind, but for their alien friends and allies. He couldn't stop thinking about it. This whole adventure still seemed surreal, and the implications of what was about to happen were at once humbling and completely mind-blowing.

"Well, you'd better believe it," Kristen grumbled, "and we've got to get up in six hours. Do you really want to fall asleep at the wheel on the single most momentous day in human history? Take a chill pill."

She meant that literally. Chill Pills were the name they cheekily gave to the med pills designed to assist with conditions on the planet. Even after ten years, the human body still needed some adjustment. Future generations would be born here and would adapt quicker. An extra dosage had the effect of mild sedation, just enough to allow some rest. But Henry didn't want to rest. He looked with envy at his partner, already snoozing, oblivious to the monumental events that were about to unfold. Her chest rose slightly with each breath, occasionally broken by a mild snort, followed by a slight movement, then settled down to repeat the cycle a few minutes later. Kristen could sleep through anything.

He got up and showered. There was no point in even trying to sleep now. The excitement and anticipation were exponentially building inside him to a point where he almost couldn't breathe. The warm water was calming, the slight difference in gravity still enough to make the sensation of water hitting the skin feel oddly pleasurable. The only sounds were the soft hissing of the showerhead, and the droplets splashing on the floor of the shower pod. He just stood there, not moving, letting the water run over his face, and for once in the last twenty-four hours, everything slowed down. He finished, dried off, and threw on a robe. It was old and worn; luxury items of clothing were not a priority here. There was little time for such frivolity when all you could think about was completing your life's work and creating a new world.

Earth seemed so far away now, both in distance and time—a dim memory reduced to a glowing pinhole in the sky, visible only through the most powerful telescopes. This was home now, and always would be. How could he possibly go back? The politics, the wars, the pollution, the sheer arrogance of a race that would surely have destroyed itself had the visitors not come all those years ago... Of course, there was always the danger that the same could happen here, but he liked to hope that humanity would reach a new level of understanding of the universe they lived in, that the sheer scope of it all would make them realise just how insignificant their petty desires were.

He looked in the mirror, wiping the steam with his hand in a waving motion. His reflection stared back: older, greyer, balder. The years here had taken their toll, but it would all be worth it. He decided to take a walk, and threw on his coveralls and boots. He looked at Kristen and thought better of waking her. He would leave quietly and come back in an hour or so. He picked up his key card and walked to the door, reaching for the handle, and slamming into it with a loud curse as it didn't open.

"Damn it," he grumbled. "What the hell is going on here?"

He tried the lock switch, tapping it furiously, but nothing happened. The door wouldn't budge. He pulled out his tablet and tried to access the facility map, but it just glowed red with the words *Access Denied* appearing in both languages. He tapped helplessly at the glass screen, but nothing happened. After about thirty seconds, the screen changed and a familiar face appeared on a video link.

"Henry."

It was Acir—at least, that was the closest he could get to pronouncing his name properly—his Efiri friend and collaborator since the project began. Even through the translator, his name was a tricky one to get right. Henry ended up calling him Ace, much to his disdain at the start; but he eventually got used to it.

"Hey Ace, what's happening? Is there something wrong?"

"Just a precaution, Henry. For your own protection. We believe a small faction of dissenters may have infiltrated the project from its initiation and are trying to sabotage it ahead of tomorrow's proceedings. The entire facility is on lockdown until the ceremony tomorrow. Please remain calm, and try to get some rest. They will be dealt with swiftly."

"Dissenters," Henry muttered. "Light years from Earth and we still can't get away from this shit. Okay, Ace, I'll sit tight until morning. See you at the ceremony."

"I—" he paused, his odd facial features contorting like only his species could, as if to say something important, but stopped himself. "I look forward to it. Good night, Henry."

The tablet blinked back to life, the door controls still locked out, but everything else functioning fine. A notification on the top of the screen indicated a new message from Steven Preston, his second in command. He tapped the icon to open it.

Henry,
We need to talk. I found something in the soil samples.
S

He attempted to reply, but apparently that network was also locked out. *What could that mean?*

He lay on the bed and opened a reading app, picking a book at random–Robert Louis Stevenson's *Kidnapped*–and began to read. He noticed a very faint odour in the air that seemed to make each breath colder, but put it down to the facility's air conditioning system, which was prone to breakdowns. After a few minutes, fatigue finally got the better of him and he dozed off, not even noticing the tablet falling out of his hand onto the soft surface of the pod floor.

II

THEY ARRIVED ON APRIL 14TH 2019 as discreetly as possible to avoid causing widespread panic. There was no single event, no fanfare or news story, no giant ships hovering over major cities. Initial contact was with the scientific community and world leaders least likely to dive into the nearest bunker in terror, who in turn, revealed the arrival of the aliens to their counterparts over an agreed period of time, building trust and eventually laying the foundations for the project.

The Efiri claimed to be from a galaxy over fifteen light years away—or as Henry liked to call it, Far, Far Away— and had travelled from their own dying world. They were roughly humanoid in shape, taller than most humans, with broader shoulders, but higher torsos, and their legs were shaped more like large insects, which gave them a somewhat comical appearance when they walked. Their skin was a very pale blue, almost translucent, and their eyes were so black you could easily get lost in them. They breathed roughly the same mixture as our own air, but were remarkably more resilient and resistant to germs and infection. As a senior NASA engineer, Henry had been one of the first to meet them, and also the first they revealed their plans to.

They had spent most of their lives travelling across the galaxy, looking for a planet they could once again call home, before finally finding somewhere suitable. They quickly revealed that it was not Earth, however, but provided coordinates for a similar planet in a neighbouring system.

So why were they here? Well, they needed help, frankly. Their numbers had dwindled, despite the advanced technology they possessed, mainly through a series of unforeseen events that could only be described as sheer bad luck. They proposed a joint venture, indeed an adventure for those who would be willing to participate. They planned to alter the planet's atmosphere slightly, over a period of ten years, using a technique they would later reveal. Despite their vast knowledge, however, there were some aspects to their anatomy that did not lend to physical strength, and one of their manufacturing methods would require some collaboration with our finest minds to perfect the necessary procedures. They wanted two thousand people to go with them and help build this new world, which would be shared equally once fully habitable. In return, they provided medical knowledge to combat most major diseases and advance the human life span by almost twenty years. Once the project was completed, they also promised to share their ship's drive technology after a significant period of assessment, and provide the means for humans to finally travel to new worlds and remove the boundaries for space exploration. It seemed like a no-brainer.

Of course, things didn't go quite to plan. The power brokers saw that they were quickly losing control of their respective populations. The revelations changed people, those who would have normally been complacent and complicit were now drunk on the endless possibilities ahead. The scramble to become one of the 2000—or the 2k, as they would come to be known—to leave Earth was unprecedented, but in truth, those needed had, for the most part, already been picked. The aliens had spent enough time studying Earth to know who the most likely candidates would be. The real problem was persuading those in power to let them go. In the end, of course, the solution was an easy one: greed. The Efiri provided enough resources and scientific advances to make those who possessed such information rich and powerful beyond any expectation they may have had before, and this provided the much-needed leverage to negotiate for the world's best and brightest.

And so it began. Exactly one year after their arrival, the aliens filled their ship with the 2k—roughly half of them scientists, the other half skilled labour, with Henry as the project leader—and prepared to leave. On the day, several terrorist attacks tried and failed to stop them. Some instigators were discovered within the group, and replaced with their alternates, who were waiting patiently for the slim chance that they might be chosen at the eleventh hour. Kristen was one of those called, and Henry had never been so grateful for terrorism.

The ship was nothing short of beautiful. Its sleek lines and metal alloy surface were so perfectly formed, it looked more like an abstract sculpture than an interstellar vessel, something moulded rather than built. The interior was equally impressive, and although not specifically designed for humans, was both comfortable and breathtaking to behold. It was like nothing anyone could ever have imagined; the entire interior seemed to be one huge interconnected honeycomb structure. The pale white surfaces of the walls were smooth, with information running constantly through visual conduits that snaked along the walls, not quite screens, but in a 3D holographic tube. Of course, the information was indecipherable, save for some familiar images that popped up every now and again, but looking at the stream was such an intense experience, it was hard to do for more than a few seconds. The ship was cramped, but the excitement of the experience kept morale high. The alien leaders appeared sporadically, whisking Henry and his senior team off for debriefings and instruction on the practices and building methods they would employ for the project. The exact methods would not be revealed until it was necessary, but the plans for building the facility were all they needed for now.

The trip that would have taken humans over a hundred years took just over three months, and upon arrival, work began immediately. The atmosphere, while quite similar to Earth, still contained trace amounts of harmful toxins that would require filtering. A simple mask would suffice for safe breathing as opposed to space suits and full breathing apparatus. Regardless, all workers wore hazmat suits for the first month as a precaution. The air was checked regularly for any danger from germs or viruses, eventually getting the all-clear. A large domed structure was quickly built to house the new arrivals, with materials crafted using state of the art 3D printing technology, enhanced tenfold by the Efiri's alterations, and habitats were fully completed within three months, during which time, they still had to live aboard the ship, shuttling to the surface every day.

The planet was half the size of Earth, and five percent of that was water. Six gargantuan air-processing plants were built over three years, spread at an equal distance across the globe. Like Earth, the planet had polar ice caps, and these were melted partially by two carefully controlled thermonuclear explosions, generating a forced air circulation which would, in tandem with the processing plants, slowly filter the entire atmosphere of the planet over a period of approximately seven years. The aliens' nuclear technology was far superior, cleaner, and more efficient than anything on Earth, as well as being much safer.

The years had gone by pretty fast. The humans eventually became accustomed to the slightly different air mixture and gravity, as well as the planet's longer days, although many did have trouble sleeping initially. There were a few isolated incidents where people just couldn't adapt mentally to the new environment, most of which sadly ended in hospitalisation and, in some cases, suicide, but the work continued. It was difficult at the best of times, even for those in the higher echelons of the human contingent. Work was equally distributed, with all doing their fair share of labour as well as the scientific and engineering work involved. This was one of the more admirable traits of the Efiri; there were few class structures, the notion of personal wealth was abhorrent to them. They thrived on having a common goal, and as soon as this was achieved, another one would be set. It was a fascinating social structure, and it did mean that they regarded humans as their lessers, but in their defence, they were in so many ways.

III

HENRY WOKE WITH A START, the nagging drone of his alarm piercing his groggy brain until he finally rose, shutting it off with a slap of his palm. Kristen was in the shower, humming an old show tune off-key, and joined him a few minutes later. A loud delivery tone sounded, and they both shuffled into the clean coveralls that appeared in the apartment's supply elevator seconds later. Hers were blue, for Science & Tech; Henry's orange, for Engineering. It had been a while since new ones had been made available, but this was the most special of occasions, and Henry wanted everything to be perfect.

The tablet chirped on the table. The red lock status changed to green, and an audible beep from the door mechanism indicated they were free to go. Henry grabbed each of them a coffee in two travel mugs, and they joined several others in the large elevator as it made its way to the surface. Excitement welled in the pit of Henry's stomach, becoming so intense he felt nauseous. Noticing his anxiety, Kristen took his hand and confidently squeezed it. He took a deep breath as the elevator reached the top floor, opening with a metallic rattle, then he and the others spilled forth into the giant hall.

The Great Hall was the one area of the installation that the aliens had built themselves, citing their own ancient traditions when questions were raised. Up to this point, no human had set foot in it. It was an enormous, ornately decorated area, very much in contrast to the interior of their ship. Two large rectangular assembly areas ran from end to end, split by a gleaming metal walkway. As they entered the hall through the huge, obsidian-coloured doors, Henry noticed Acir on the other side of the room and called to him, but he didn't respond. Henry was sure Acir saw him, but he just blanked him and continued walking to the front of the hall.

The Efiri guards ushered the humans to one side of the hall, while the Efiri occupied the other, separated by the three-foot-high walkway. While the humans looked to their counterparts to share their excitement at the finalisation of this wonderful project, their looks were not met. The aliens stood rigid, staring forward in perfect formation. As the remaining humans scuttled to their area, the enormous doors began to close. Outside the dome, the sun had risen, and newly formed clouds tumbled majestically across the off-blue sky. That air would soon be breathable, those clouds would soon drench the landscape with refreshing, life-giving rain, and they made this happen.

A large stage stood at the front of the hall, with a wide lectern protruding from the floor. The alien leader, known as The Exemplar—a large individual much older in appearance than the others—shuffled forward, flanked by two others, and although the alien's expressions were hard to read, it was clear his was far too solemn for the occasion. Something was off.

Henry and Kristen stood at the front of the crowd. As the leader of the 2k, he had expected to be asked to join them on the stage, to celebrate the occasion, but obviously that wasn't going to happen. Confusion gave way to suspicion as people looked to Henry for some sort of explanation.

Kristen tapped his shoulder. "Where's Stephen? I can't see him anywhere."

Henry shrugged, placing his hand in his overall pocket. As he did, he felt something inside. It was a piece of paper. He took it out and unfolded it, recognising the handwriting as Stephen's. As he read, Henry took a step backward, reeling from shock, grabbing Kristen's arm to steady himself. The colour completely drained from his face.

"What is it, Henry?"

He passed the note to her.

Henry,
This world, they killed it. The samples matched. It's all a lie.

Stephen had been researching the planet's soil and found a strange residual signature in the samples. It wasn't until the samples returned from the sites of the detonations at the poles that he realised that the low level radioactive signature matched those of the alien weapons. They had originally destroyed this planet.

A loud klaxon interrupted the chatter of the crowd as The Exemplar spoke, his voice amplified and translated for all to hear in a flat, synthesised accent, one terrifying word:

"Goodbye."

For once in his life, Henry had no idea what to do. As he looked up, he saw Ace standing beside his leader, staring directly at him.

He knows. That bastard knows.

A loud mechanical noise came from the floor beneath them as it shook, throwing some off balance while others clung to those nearest to steady themselves. The entire floor on the human side of the hall began to descend. Widespread panic erupted. Some desperately tried to clamber up the rising wall, but they were quickly pushed back down by alien guards falling on those below them. People ran around what little space there was, frantically looking for escape, but there was none. They piled on top of each other, desperately trying to climb higher, but the floor kept descending faster than they could climb. There was no way out. Some fell to their knees, wailing uncontrollably as the floor juddered to a stop after about fifty feet. The walls were completely smooth, without apertures of any kind. People grabbed each other for comfort, crying into each other's shoulders, while others turned to anger, swearing uncontrollably at the aliens above, some going so far as removing shoes and throwing them upward as hard as possible. It was all in vain, of course. There was nothing anyone could do. Henry stood still, staring blankly at the piece of paper. Earth had probably met the same fate as this planet already had, and the aliens would soon trawl the galaxy once again, looking for the next bunch of gullible natives to coerce and conquer.

At the surface, a loud altercation seemed to be taking place. It was hard to discern from all the noise below, but there was definitely a human involved. There was a loud scream, followed by a weapon discharge, and seconds later, a body was hurled over the edge, almost landing on a group cowering together. They managed to sidestep just in time as the listless body struck the ground with a sickening, bone-crunching noise. It was Stephen. He was already dead before he hit the ground, the blackened stain of a pulse blast across his chest.

The others looked to him, each terrified face pleading for an explanation. But what could he do?

A loud, shuddering mechanical noise came from the surface as a large platform drew itself across the opening above. This caused even more panic as the movement of the enormous cover began to block out the light. Within a minute, the final sliver of light at the edge disappeared as the opening sealed, and the entire area was plunged into an inky, total darkness. The finality of this was both overwhelming and claustrophobic, the final lid on the coffin of humanity. All they could hope for now was that it would be quick, that their captors would give them the parting gift of a painless death. He knew now that this was the reason humans were not allowed to participate in the construction of the Great Hall. This was no collaboration, and it was obvious now that the Efiri had no intention of sharing this planet.

Three small circles appeared, equidistant along the length of the roof now covering them, pale orange in colour. Seconds later, another concentric circle appeared outside each circle, each a paler hue than the last, followed by four more. As the last circle appeared, a deep thrumming sound came from the floor, so heavy that Henry's teeth chattered from the vibration. The frequency of the sound rose, and as it did, the brightness of the rings intensified. As the sound and brightness reached critical, Henry and Kristen embraced tearfully, so tightly it felt as if they could never let go, because they both knew they would never have to.

IV
EARTH-FIVE YEARS LATER.

THE NEWS ANCHOR SITS NERVOUSLY in his seat as the make-up artist touches up his face. A little stubble is beginning to break through, which doesn't make her job any easier, but he's been awake for almost twenty-four hours straight, and at this point he really doesn't care. She does her best, and he does his best not to swear profusely at her.

The director ushers her off the set as the countdown to a live broadcast begins and the key lights brighten on the news desk. The anchor adjusts his hair in a hand-held mirror, a task that by now he has timed to the millisecond. His sullen appearance transforms to that of a consummate professional, his whitened teeth bordering on the ridiculous against the contrast of his heavily-tanned face as the ten-second countdown reaches the muted final two seconds and the broadcast begins.

"Welcome to ISN National News Network. We interrupt your regular programming for an important news bulletin."

A pulsing, hideously-designed, animated graphic appears in a rectangle to the left of his head proclaiming some Breaking News.

"We go live now to Washington, where an unprecedented event has taken place. We can reveal that the Efiri have returned. Their ship is currently in orbit, and several of their shuttles have now landed nearby. It has been almost fifteen years since the group known as the 2k left with them, and this is the first contact we've had with them since. We can confirm that the President has met with the alien leaders and a press conference is about to take place."

The camera switches to the live feed from the White House, showing an apprehensive president standing beside The Exemplar. A gaggle of eager reporters jostle each other for space, cameras and devices held high in an effort to find a free line of sight. It's the first time this president has met with the aliens, and most of the people who dealt with them fifteen years ago have either moved on or are dead. Truth be told, no one expected them to come back. He clears his throat and speaks.

"My fellow citizens: I stand here today at this unprecedented event to welcome the Efiri back to our home. As you know, almost fifteen years ago, the aliens visited us to propose a collaboration between our peoples, a group was picked to join them on their project to reclaim and revive a habitable planet. I hand you over now to The Exemplar for an update."

The Exemplar moves into position as the president steps aside, and speaks through his translator.

"People of Earth, we thank you for once more welcoming us to your planet. I am sure you are all curious as to the result of our project. I can reveal to you that is was a resounding success. Our human colleagues made an invaluable contribution, and are currently living happily with their counterparts on Riva-6. You may ask why none of the original 2k have joined us on this journey, and the explanation is simple: we are not returning to Riva-6. A second project has been established with the same goal as previously. We have identified another planet and will replicate the initiative on this planet also. We have refined the process even further, and we wish to announce that once again, we have requested another contingent to collaborate with us. We have spent the past four weeks contacting and recruiting all potential candidates already and they are gathered here today."

The Exemplar steps away as the president takes the podium once more. A large curtain opens and the camera pans out to reveal the large group standing to one side.

"Thank you, Exemplar. This is truly a momentous day in our history. To all potential candidates, I have this to say: I am in awe and equally envious of the adventure about to begin for you all. Mankind has truly evolved so that one day soon, we hope that we may even get to visit our friends on these planets. For now, though, we must watch and support a new team as they represent the human race beyond our galaxy."

He leans forward, grasping each side of the lectern with both hands, and turns his head to the new recruits.

"Welcome, to the new 2k."

~*~

Mary Janes on the Moon
Jessica West

~*~

ALICE STEPPED ONTO THE COBBLESTONE STREET in front of the orphanage. Her Mary Janes clicked and clacked. She shivered, rubbing her arms for warmth.

She stopped next to her heap of rusty luggage. Someone had opened a window facing Hope Street where she stood. Her stomach grumbled at the smell wafting out to greet her—a fresh strawberry cake—even though she'd just had breakfast moments before they'd put her out for good.

She pulled out a small, silver canteen and unscrewed the cap. Years of use had worn her father's name all but away. Well, she'd assumed it was her father's name. They'd gotten separated in that final moment on Earth, when the shuttles filled rapidly and it was every man for himself.

She'd given up hope long ago, in her darkest night when she'd accidentally set her best friend on fire. The other kids made fun of her. Said she'd wet the bed if she kept playing with fire. How often had she wished that was the worst that could happen?

Alice poured gasoline onto the heap of luggage, and tossed the canteen onto it as well. She lit a match, and left another past behind.

~*~

Patient Zero
Rhett C. Bruno

~*~

THE COUGHING STARTED ON MY THIRD DAY crammed into the packed cargo-hold of a shipping freighter bound for New Terra. Of course, that didn't mean I'd finally contracted the Rusina Plague. A cough could be attributed to a great many causes, right? For starters, I wasn't used to being in zero-g, I had limited water supply, and the air blowing through the recyclers was characteristically stale for a cheap ship.

After a week, my throat was so dry and scratchy that I wanted to shove my hand down it and claw just to earn a second of relief. Still, I didn't want to jump to conclusions. In the back of my mind, a part of me had always wondered if I was somehow immune. Maybe that was how I lasted so long when so many of the others around me got ill.

By the two-week mark, I was starving. All I'd managed to bring with me were a few yeasty ration bars, but no matter how hungry I was, when I tried to shove even the smallest piece into my mouth, it came up immediately in the form of vomit. Probably because they had the texture of paste and were essentially tasteless. What I wouldn't have given for a sip of cold ale back at the tavern in Purgat City.

A day later, my stomach was at war with itself and I gave up entirely on eating. There weren't any supplies nearby to clean up with and the hold was beginning to smell dreadful.

There was no more denying it.

Intense nausea was the second noticeable symptom of the plague. I had it. Slowly and surely, it was going to eat away at my organs until I'd need to be hooked up to a machine just to continue drawing breath. Then, like every patient on Rusina before me, I would die an agonizing death.

I stared out into space through the tiny porthole sunken into the cargo hold's back wall. My eyelids were as heavy as steel shutters from not being able to sleep, so even doing that took a great deal of effort. A teeming array of stars raced by like strings of light as the freighter zoomed along through space at unconscionable speeds. They'd lost much of their luster to me. After countless hours drifting around alongside my own foul stench and floating bile, it was hard to find the beauty in anything.

The exit ramp's controls winked at me. For hours I'd been going back and forth on whether or not I should unseal it and allow the great vacuum to cleanse the ship of both myself and the plague I carried. It was the right thing to do, wasn't it?

The right thing to do, I scoffed to myself. I wasn't sure what was right anymore. All I could do was force myself to picture my wife's decaying body, and remember why I'd climbed onto a freighter bound for the most populated world in the sector in the first place...

~*~

"You should leave, Des," my wife, Alora, said to me a day before I found myself alone in space. The intercom on my side of a glass divider transmitted her frail, gravelly voice.

"Leave?" I replied. It was always hard to keep my voice from cracking while seeing her so weak.

"I mean this planet—Rusina."

I sighed. Every day or so it was the same thing. She'd tell me in some way or another that I should go far away and start fresh. I suppose it was kind of her, but I wasn't going to give up on her and I wasn't going to leave her alone on Rusina, no matter how much she begged.

"Don't start this again," I said.

As soon as those words left my lips, Alora began coughing. She turned away and bent over so I wouldn't be able to hear it clearly through the intercom. It didn't work. The struggle of her lungs was evident and before long, she was gagging on air. There was nothing left inside of her to regurgitate. No matter how many times I'd heard the sound, it still made me cringe. By the time she was finally able to withdraw her skinny arm from her mouth, she was laboring to breath.

"Everyone else is going," she said as if nothing had happened.

"Everyone who can afford it," I grumbled. "C'mon, Alora, you know I'm not just going to leave you here alone. Give up on it already."

Her thin, dry lips curled into a faint smile. *That smile*. I could remember it from the moment we met clear as day. Her cheeks were rosier then, and her body fuller. What a beauty she'd been. I swear she could've modeled back on one of the core planets if she wasn't so modest. But the

Rusina Plague had spent the last eight months ravaging her body. Now she was all skin and bones.

"If you stop paying for me you can sell our farm-grid. That should be enough to get you passage and a new apartment on one of the core worlds…where things are less rural. You'll be happy there. You can—"

"I'm not leaving you," I said firmly. "Besides, I'm barely paying for your care as it is. They're so many of you in here that all the nurses who haven't left are pretty much volunteers, same as you were. Bless their souls."

Because her face was so gaunt, it was hard to tell her exact reaction to my response just by looking. After ten years of marriage, however, I knew she was at the very least disappointed. "Just think about it, alright? Can't get much worse in here anyway."

"As long as you promise to keep fighting. There'll be someone out there who can help us find a cure soon. I'm sure of it. The New Terra Council should be answering our request for aid any day now."

"Always the optimist." She raised her hand to place it against the glass, clenching her jaw the entire time she did as if even that small task was a struggle.

I pressed my palm against hers, the transparent surface separating us by the widest inch I could fathom. We held them there for as long as possible—a minute, maybe two, I don't know. It was until her arm started shaking from holding it up, which was hardly long enough for me.

That was the closest we could get to touching for a little over eight months. The Rusina Plague was extremely contagious and transmitted through contact. Alora caught it while working as a volunteer nurse after the outbreak. She was as careful as anyone, but even that wasn't enough. Sometimes I thought about signing up just so I could get in and sit with her without glass between us, but she didn't want me to. To be honest, I didn't have the stomach for it, either. Wearing a hazmat suit seemed as impersonal as glass anyway, and I was never as courageous as she was.

"Would you mind," she said before hesitating. Her expression darkened and she stared straight into my eyes. I could tell immediately that my least favorite part of every day was coming early. "Letting me get some rest?"

"Already? It's still early." I glanced down at my hand terminal. There was no service down in the quarantine buried a hundred feet beneath the surface of Rusina, but the time only read 4:37 PM, New Terra time. I usually got her until visiting hours ended at five.

"I know, I'm sorry... I just haven't been getting much sleep lately."

It was always hard for me to look at her and not envision her how she was before the plague hit, but she did look exhausted. Her eyes were red as cool fire and the dark rings beneath them sagged as much as her tight skin would allow.

"It's fine," I exhaled. "I'm just being selfish. I have to go meet Braxx anyway. Shipments go out tomorrow and we had a great harvest this month. I'm hoping to get a few more credits than usual. But I'll be back first thing tomorrow."

Her lips began to tremble, but she steadied them enough to speak. "You really don't have to keep coming back every day, Des," she said. "I wouldn't blame you."

I forced a grin. "I know that, but I look forward to it every time I wake up. I promise."

"Okay..." she muttered. I expected my response to at least make her face brighten a little, but all it managed to accomplish was getting her to turn her despondent gaze away from me.

"I'll give Braxx your best," I said. "One day I'll get him to come see you." I placed my fingers against the glass again. She didn't have the energy left to do the same. "I love you. More than anything."

"I love you too." She was seized by another racking bout of coughs. This time she didn't bother to let it pass. She just got up and shuffled away without looking back.

I lingered for a few seconds while a man with the same affliction came limping in to take her place behind the glass. He was in even worse condition. His sallow flesh was stippled with grotesque, open sores from head to toe. The nurses tried their best to hide them with cover-up, but they were amateurs. Judging by how excruciatingly visible his ribs were through the baggy medical gown he was wearing, the poor man couldn't have had more than week left.

Alora was wrong. It could get much worse. I had to get her out.

I stood up and walked away like I always did, my legs feeling like jelly. The head nurse, Resa, patted me on the back as I left. No words were necessary between us. She was a lovely woman once, tall and confident, but the outbreak had given her creases and doubts just like it had everyone else.

She sent me along and called up the next sorry Rusinan to replace me in the visiting rooms. There were at least twenty others waiting in line, from a handful of the many different species living together on Rusina. Some were crying…newcomers. The rest of us had spilled all our tears by then. We all held the same blank, defeated stare. As if the answer to our problems was somewhere far, far beyond the edge of sight. I nodded at them and they nodded back, but their stares never shifted. Such was life on Rusina after the plague hit.

~*~

It was nearly dusk when I emerged from the quarantine hidden deep beneath Purgat, the only city on Rusina. The streets threading between its dense cluster of gleaming towers were barren like always. Barely even a hover-car in sight. Metal everywhere was beginning to rust and decay. The glare of the sun barely penetrated the dust-covered glass of tower windows. Like its people, Purgat was fading. The population dropped daily, whether it was from people dying of disease or finally saving up enough credits to leave for good.

It wasn't always that way. When Tenaris Corp, the wealthiest corporation in the sector, discovered Rusina on the outer rim of civilized space, they hastily funded the development of the colony. With no intelligent, indigenous fauna to worry about, as well as a temperate climate suited for farming, it was a perfect location for them to expand operations. They were setting up a new headquarters in the star system over and it needed plenty of food to sustain it.

They looked for anyone to immigrate, even people from beyond the Terra Republic. In exchange, you'd receive a sizeable farming plot and free residence in a shiny, new city. Alora and I—newly married and madly in love—took the deal without thinking twice. It was our ticket out of the slums of New Terra. Millions of others made the same choice. Anything Tenaris Corp needed we grew in bulk, and they paid us well for tending our plots.

For a while, it was the best decision we ever made. Rusina was far away from all the Republic's wars and politics, so we had no problems. It was a peaceful place. I used to stroll around Purgat and see children playing— humans with humans, humans with aliens, it didn't matter. Nobody cared what species their neighbors were so long as they did their jobs and stayed out of trouble.

For seven flawless years it went on like that before we discovered we weren't alone on Rusina. Nobody knows where or when it started exactly, but the plague began to spread and it didn't discriminate. Every sentient species was in danger. Now, seeing even a single child was like seeing a character out of one of Earth's long-forgotten myths. Any parent with a brain was smart enough to send their kids far, far away. I was just happy that Alora and I decided not to have one.

Tenaris Corp had the resources to help, but they quickly found another planet on which to grow their crops and backed out, leaving us alone to convince the great and powerful Terra Republic to consider sending aid to a meager farming colony out in the middle of dead space. They'd never bothered to answer. Every day I told Alora that help was coming, and every day it broke me a little bit more to lie. We were truly alone in our fight, with neither the means nor skills to find a cure for what was killing us.

"How is she?" a voice asked.

I jumped. I was so deep in thought I'd made it halfway across Purgat completely unaware. I turned around to see Braxx standing outside of Paradise Tavern, a sharp-toothed grin plastered on his big, scaly face. He was a Krell—a reptilian, bipedal species fairly new to the Republic. Normally, his back was hunched so we were about the same height, but on those rare occasions when he felt threatened and straightened out, he was easily two feet taller. That wasn't even counting the long tail sloshing about on the ground behind him.

"The same," I said. "You know you can come down and see her sometime if you'd like?"

"I'd rather not see her like this, but I beg the Great Hunter to spare her nightly," he said. Krell had a difficult time using their voices to illustrate any range of emotion when they were speaking outside of their native tongue. The extreme, palatal lisp caused by their long tongues made English difficult for them. I knew he was being genuine, however. Braxx was the closest friend I had left on Rusina.

"I won't force you, but you know she misses you."

"And I miss her too." His big, wide-set eyes blinked once then he turned and gestured toward the crooked sign above the tavern. "You look like you could use a drink."

I chuckled. Krell weren't generally good at emotions. They were a species of hunters who weren't around long enough to have evolved far—by societal standards that is—before the Terra Republic lifted them to intelligent status. I didn't mind. He was easy to talk to.

I wrapped my arm around his broad shoulders, grinned, and said, "Try ten."

~*~

Paradise Tavern was fairly packed. It was the only bar on Rusina still operational. The place had a sort of charming, old-world feel. There was a four-armed Velaren playing away at a Velaren Organ—similar to a piano, but with two stacked rows of keys—in the corner. Such a magnificent harmony had no place in a world so brimming with despair.

We passed through the makeshift decontamination chamber at the door, the same kind placed at the entrance of every building in Purgat. They didn't always catch everything, but it helped make us feel safer. It beeped that we were clean, and we took a seat at the bar.

I ordered a beer, Braxx got vodka. Both were free. Rusina had such a surplus of produce after Tenaris Corp left that there wasn't really a reason to charge. A robot bartender placed both beverages down. I decided to put in my order for a second one straight away. Just to be efficient. The bot was an older Tenaris model, so it wasn't very fast. At least *it* was immune to sickness. A part of me resented the tin can for that.

"Shipments going out tomorrow, eh?" I asked Braxx once we were settled in. I took a lengthy sip of my drink, almost draining half the glass all at once it was so refreshing. If there was one thing we did right on Rusina, it was brewing.

"At noon," Braxx replied. "You've had the haulers bring in your harvest already, right?" He began lapping at his glass with his forked tongue. After ten years of friendship it didn't faze me at all, but I imagine people from the more human-centric areas of the Republic might've taken offense. They could be so stuffy on core worlds.

"Of course. The whole eastern grid had a great yield. You still planning on asking the Republic for a few more credits?"

"If it comes up."

"Oh c'mon, Braxx. What can it hurt? We can all use the credits, otherwise this city's going to rust away."

"You know they don't like bargaining with independent traders."

I sighed. As much as I loved Braxx, for the life of me I never understood why Tenaris Corp hired a Krell to run Rusina's shipping station. They were about as good with commerce as they were with feelings.

"Trust me, I know," I said. "For the last three years I've been begging the council for help. One real doctor or scientist or anything and we might be able to figure out a cure. Three fuckin' years, Braxx, and I can't even get a damned hearing. *We are reviewing your case and will schedule a hearing at our earliest possible convenience.* That's the best I ever get. I know they've got their war and all but…man." My fist slammed down on the counter so hard that it startled the Krell and almost caused him to knock over his glass with his tongue. "I'm sure if something like this happened at New Terra, they'd get it cleaned up in a week."

Braxx shrugged his broad shoulders. His best attempt at displaying emotion. "Do you expect anything different from them?"

"I expect—" I began before biting back the words and taking a deep breath. At some point during our conversation, my beer had wound up empty. I picked up my second and, after realizing how good an idea it was to have it handy, signaled the robot for another.

"I expect at least an answer," I said. "Farmers, engineers, or whatever, there are still a million people on Rusina. Good, hardworking people. We don't deserve this."

Braxx patted me on the back and turned to look me straight in the face with the thin, vertical pupils of his lizard-like eyes. "Nobody does. We'll figure it out, Desmond. Plenty of Rusinans have been down there much longer than her. We have time."

"That's what everyone keeps telling me. I just wish there was something I could do besides sending out messages that nobody important will ever read."

As soon as I stopped speaking, a loud, grating cough echoed from somewhere in the Tavern. It definitely wasn't just from liquid going down the wrong pipe. The Velaren Organ trailed off on a few wrong notes, and the room got so quiet I could hear the engine of the robot bartender whirring through his rusty chassis. After a few more seconds, the coughing continued, louder and throatier than before.

The robot's pale eye-lenses went red and an alarm sounded throughout the tavern. "Possible contaminant present, please evacuate the building," it repeated between every wail.

Nobody wasted any time before hurrying for the exit. Even Braxx and I were halfway out the door before I remembered that I forgot to grab my drink.

The entrance to the tavern sealed behind us. Everyone who was healthy stood outside in the brisk air, and the poor man who'd coughed stood inside. He had only the bartender to keep him company. The cough could've derived from something as harmless as breathing in too much dirt out on his farm, but taking risks, even with something as insignificant as that, was a thing of the past.

The distant cries of sirens grew louder, and I could see the flashing red lights of two hover-cars weaving their way through the valleys of rusting towers. We had no proper police force on Rusina. There wasn't any need for one. But after the outbreak, hospital workers put together a hazard squad using what little tech Tenaris Corp Security left behind.

"Figures," I said. "Can't even get drunk these days."

"You can come back to my place," Braxx suggested. "I've got a fresh bottle of Krell Mash I snatched up last time I was on New Terra. It's strong."

"Maybe... I was planning to go check on my plot later tonight. Make sure the equipment is right and ready to start on the next harvest. Get some fresh air."

Braxx snickered. Well, it was closer to a hiss coming from his Krell snout, but I knew his intent. "We'll bring it there, then."

~*~

Neither Braxx nor I were probably in the best state to drive a hover-car, but we made it to my plot safe enough. There wasn't much traffic on Rusina, after all. I parked on top of a thick watering line. My land was directly beneath us, buzzing drones carefully planting its new seeds. Other than keeping up the equipment, mostly everything was automated. Sometimes Alora and I liked to turn it all off and till the soil ourselves like they did in ancient times. Since she went away, however, I hadn't even attempted that. It reminded me too much of days when she could run.

"Here," Braxx said after we got out of the vehicle.

He handed me the half-empty bottle of the blue liquid he called Krell Mash. It tasted like shit on fire, but by that point I didn't care. I plopped down on the hood of the hover-car and took a swig. Braxx snickered in his usual manner when I wrinkled my face and handed it back.

"How do you people drink that?" I asked, gasping for air.

"We need flavor. You humans wouldn't understand." He stuck his long tongue inside the bottle to fish out some Krell Mash. Again, I didn't mind. All I had to worry about was the plague, and we both would've known if either of us had it.

I nudged him in the arm and begged for the bottle. The next sip made my toes tingle. I gave it back and stared straight out across Rusina.

A few miles away, Purgat glistened like a string of pearls against the night sky. Somehow it made the two moons above pale in comparison. Between us and it was an endless quilt of farms extending in every direction. A grid of raised, industrial watering lines separated each plot, and tremendous glass shields made each segment appear like a precious jewelry box harboring emeralds.

"Beautiful, isn't it?" I said.

"Used to be brighter," Braxx replied matter-of-factly.

"There used to be more of us to turn on the lights." I lay back and looked up at the stars. "You know you're the only one still on this planet with a working interstellar ship, right?"

"It's not actually mine. I'm still working to pay off Tenaris Corp for it."

"True… but you could take it wherever you want, sell it for scraps and disappear. It's a piece of junk anyway. They'd probably never even try to look for you."

Braxx bore his sharp teeth and glared in my direction. "Junk?"

"Oh, you know what I mean. Outdated, to them at least. You could leave all this behind while you're still healthy."

Braxx shrugged. "Where would I go? This is my home now."

"Anywhere! You could make a new home. It may not look as pretty as this one, but at least it'll be full of life. You won't have to watch your neighbors disappear. You won't look up and see a sky empty of ships. You won't have to send your wife…" I swallowed. Maybe the liquor was loosening up my tears ducts, but before I could stop myself I began to weep. Braxx put his arm around me and pulled me close.

"I should be in there with her," I sniveled. "If I wasn't wasting my time out here drinking away my sorrows I could've been there helping her with the new patients. Maybe if I'd been there to look over her hazmat suit once more, it wouldn't have been comprised."

"You've been doing this to yourself for eight months, Des. It's not your fault. We all dealt with the outbreak in our own way. I used to circle the planet twice when I got back from delivering a shipment, just to think about things. I didn't know what else to do. Every time I'd consider turning around, but after a while, I'd wind up descending and go back to my life like nothing had changed."

I was surprised by his answer. He always seemed so calm and collected. I never could even read the inner turmoil written on his face which beset so many people on Rusina. "Why?" I asked.

"I've seen plenty of other worlds. My people inhabit the slums on many, or are forced to serve in the military. If I am to succumb to the Great Hunter, I'd rather it be on Rusina than in any of those places. The people here have been kind to me."

"You, Krell." I managed to force a narrow grin. We all had our own reasons for staying, and his was so pure it almost made me feel foolish. "Well, I hope the Hunter never finds you, my friend."

"He finds us all, eventually." He lifted the bottle of Krell Mash to his lips and slurped some down. "Have you ever thought about leaving?"

"Of course. Every night when the lights go out and my mind is free to wander, I consider what it might be like not to have to live in fear every minute. Then I see Alora again and remember why I can't. Not until I find some way to treat her."

"I understand." Braxx put on his best smirk, which often times just made him look angry with his multitude of skinny, sharp teeth. "You could take her with you, you know. Drop her at the foot of some genius doctor on New Terra and tell him to figure it out or die."

My eyes widened. I couldn't believe I'd never thought of that before. It was genius, really. The people of New Terra had figured out how to travel across stars. They'd settled the galaxy from old Earth to the far, outermost rim. Surely, they could cure just one disease on one small planet before it was able to spread throughout their worlds? "That's not the worst idea I've heard," I said.

"I was making a joke," Braxx said. Even with his minor vocal inflections I could tell he was shocked by my response.

"Oh... right. Me too." I sat up and pointed to the bottle of blue liquor he was hogging. "Hand that over." When I took a drink that time, I didn't even flinch.

~*~

I awoke the next morning to the beeping of the communications console in my apartment in Purgat. My head was pounding. I took some minor painkillers and cleared it up in a hurry. Thinking too much made my head ache every morning, so I'd pretty much gotten addicted to the things since Alora got sick.

I glanced over at my console, wishing it would shut up just so I could get a few more minutes of sleep. Then I remembered it'd been set to only alert me about a response to the most recent message I'd sent to the New Terra council. Anything that had to do with Alora specifically would come right through my hand terminal.

I jumped out of bed and hurried over to it. I tried to tell myself not to expect anything, but that didn't keep my heart from racing. I sat down, switched on the screen, and signed in to my Terra-net account. It was from the Terra Republic Council's Office, as expected.

Dear Mr. Barlow,

We are still reviewing your case and will schedule a hearing at our earliest possible convenience.

My shoulders sagged. If I could've cried sober I would have. It always took three months to get a response from them, and every three months since I'd begun querying them I got the same message. If an automated response was still considered polite on the core worlds, then I could easily understand why Braxx had no desire to leave for one.

I shook my head to wipe that thought before I copied back the same urgent message I'd sent to them previously. I clicked resend so hard that I cracked the screen. In another three months, Alora might be gone and I had little doubt I'd get anything but the same reply by then, but it was the only thing I could do short of attending medical university for ten years and discovering a cure for myself.

My hands trembled as I sat, staring at the damaged screen in silence. 12:23 PM, New Terra time. Visiting hours at the quarantine started at one. There wasn't even enough time to get a bite to eat if I wanted to beat the crowds. I found if I kept Alora on a strict schedule of being awake at the same time every day, she was always feeling a little better and more willing to talk. I won't lie and say it didn't help me either.

One o'clock. That was Alora's time, from then until the sun started falling.

~*~

The message from the council's office had me too frustrated to think clearly. I got off at the wrong stop on the Purgat Interloop and had to double back on foot just to make up time. It was 1:12 p.m. when I finally hopped onto the lift down into the quarantine alongside at least a dozen other unfortunate visitors. A few were new, but most were faces I'd seen out of the corner of my vision time and time again, like characters in a bad dream.

The waiting room was more packed than usual. I sat for an hour with nothing to do but twiddle my thumbs. When my session finally arrived, head nurse Resa came walking out of confinement, her whole body slouching. She passed through the decontamination chamber and stepped out of her hazmat suit before heading over to me. She wore an even more somber look than usual.

"Hi, Desmond," she said. "Alora had a rough night. She told me she'd rather not get out of bed. Can you come back later? I'm sure she'll be more up to it."

"I know I'm late, but tell her it won't be for long," I responded. I knew I was being selfish, but after my night with Braxx and the council's non-response, I needed to see her. I needed a reminder of why I couldn't leave Rusina. "She should try to walk a little, right?"

"Desmond, she'll still be here tomorrow. Don't worry."

"I know that. I just want to see her for a second."

She placed one of her long-fingered hands on my chest and looked me straight in the eyes. "It might be good for you to get out. How many days has it been since you didn't see her?"

I knew that answer without even having to think. "Seventy-one."

"If only my husband were that dedicated," Resa mused, but clearly didn't get the reaction she expected. She cleared her throat. "You'll drive yourself mad if you don't take some time to yourself. Go tend the farm, or take a drive out beyond the farm-grids. I hear the mountains up north are beautiful. You come back in a few days and I'll have her all fed, cleaned up, and looking lovely as ever. How does that sound?"

"Is that your advice or hers?" I asked, a harsh edge creeping into my voice. I wished I could take it back.

Resa removed her hand from me and frowned. "She just needs some time alone," she said. "Look, I've got to take care of something, but I'll message you straight away when she's feeling better."

I bit out the angry words percolating in my throat. It wasn't Resa's fault, but I was tired of waiting on messages. "Yeah...thanks," I grumbled.

She offered me a faint smile before continuing on to speak with another sorry visitor. I went to turn around and leave, but as I did I caught a glimpse of her hazmaat suit sitting in a tub right outside the decontamination chamber. Her containment key-card was dangling from her pocket on a lanyard. There was a surveillance camera, but there'd been no one around to man security for months. Who was foolish enough to want to sneak into the quarantine ward anyway?

Throughout the minute I stood there silently, I must have told myself *no* a thousand times. That Alora just needed some time alone.

It didn't work.

As hard as this was for her, it was hard for me too. All I wanted was to wrap my arms around her so I knew we were both still in the fight together. She was a nurse for over two years before she contracted the plague. Surely, I'd be safe beyond containment for a couple of minutes?

I looked around. Everyone in the waiting area was too preoccupied to notice me. The nurses had stepped into a private office for a conference.

I strolled leisurely toward the decontamination chamber, holding my breath as I did. Once there, I quickly slipped into Resa's hazmat suit. It was tight, but I was able to get it around my stocky frame after a few tugs. I picked up the bulbous helmet sitting nearby and lowered it down over my head.

I thoroughly checked all of the seals. I'd helped Alora put hers on plenty of times back in the day so I knew what I was doing. Once I was sure it was okay, I swiped Resa's keycard in front of the scanner and stepped into the chamber. The outer seal slammed shut and then a tight grid of pink-hued beams traced lines through and around me. It gave my whole body a tingle.

"Decontamination complete," a robotic voice chimed as the inner seal opened.

I was in. All those years watching Alora go in and out, and I'd finally mustered the courage to do it for myself.

"Out of the way!" A Krell nurse hissed, almost knocking me over.

He and another were rushing along with a hovering gurney. There was a young human girl lying on top, her body writhing violently. She was the first child I'd seen on Rusina in more time than I cared to count. She couldn't have been older than eight. Her legs were so puny that they were like sticks blowing in the wind. Her howl was earsplitting even through my helmet and the short glimpse I got of her lesion-covered face had my stomach turning. She didn't just look like she was in agony. She looked terrified, like she knew her time had come but she wasn't ready.

I held the contents of my stomach down and hurried down the hall. Screams echoed from behind every room I passed. Dozens of them. Each one had a name card on the door. The nurses didn't even bother to remove the ones from the room's previous occupants. They just stacked them one on top of the other.

I checked each name, searching desperately for Alora's. Every so often a nurse would go running by me toward another shriek. But as soon as they passed, another cry would ring out from the opposite direction. There weren't nearly enough caregivers.

When I finally found Alora's room, I had to stop myself from barreling through the entrance. I needed to get out of the corridor before I heard another scream. I felt like I was stuck in a nightmare. The door was unlocked. All was silent behind it. I took a deep breath and edged through quietly, making sure nobody was watching.

Alora was propped up on the bed inside, her skinny arm drooping off the edge with an IV drip stuck into it. A noisy machine at her side pumped oxygen through a respirator that was strapped to her nose. It was on wheels, but I'd never seen her with it before. I only then realized how hard it must have been for her to meet with me every day and struggle to breathe without it.

She looked up from her bed, and I swear if I was from a foreign galaxy I might not have even recognized her as human. Her hair was a tangled mess. Her eyes bulged from their sunken sockets as if they were ready to tumble out at any time. The opening down the side of her medical-gown was pulled open from how she was laying, allowing me to see every ridge of her hip and ribs. I could wrap my entire hand around her waist.

I froze in the entrance. The key-card slipped out of my grasp. The nurses must've worked hard every morning she went to see me, because she never appeared so dreadful. Her skin looked like it was ready to flake away and finally complete her transformation into a walking skeleton. A patch of rosy lesions covered her forehead.

"Des, you shouldn't be here!" she rasped before coughing. She looked horrified, probably because of the way I was staring at her. Like I'd just seen a monster.

There were no words to say. I approached her slowly, unable to peel my gaze away. I'd spent the better part of three years trying to deal with the outbreak, but only then did I realize that I'd merely been hiding from it. Every pointless message sent to the Terra Republic was just an excuse to avoid confronting it directly. Alora was in containment because she was a hero, and there I was, a coward forcing himself in just because he needed reassurance.

"Alora, I'm so sorry," I whimpered as I sat down next to her carefully, worried I might break her in half if I sat too quickly. "I should've listened to Resa."

Her thin, colorless lips somehow managed to lift into a smile. She rolled over to face me completely. My heart felt like it was going to burst through my ribs.

"Des, I…I didn't want you to see me like this," she whispered. They must have amplified her voice in the meeting room as well, because it was so feeble that I could hardly hear her. She had to take a long, labored breath between every sentence.

I wrapped my gloved hands around one of hers and pulled it close to my face. Tears began streaming down my cheeks. "I never really understood why you wanted me to leave until today," I said.

"Is that what this is about? Oh, Des, I never *wanted* you to leave. I just know that there are brighter places for you out there. I want just you to be happy."

"How could I be happy when you're trapped in here? I should be spending every day at your side, cleaning your messes… feeding you. What a fool I am."

She ran her bony finger over my visor to hush me. "I don't want that for you."

"Neither did I, but those brighter places you're talking about sent back another useless response today. They don't care about us. This is where I belong."

"Like you've said a thousand times, the council will come around."

"They won't!" I snapped. "They have their own affairs…"

I paused. The Krell Mash had helped me forget Braxx's joke from the night before, but it came rushing back to me like a brewing storm. He may've been kidding, but that didn't mean it was stupid. Bring Alora to one of their planets and drop her at the foot of a real hospital. Then see how long it took them to come up with a cure. It was that simple.

"Des?" Alora asked. She started to cough until she was pretty much gagging on phlegm.

I handed her the cloth sitting on the end of her bed to wipe her mouth with. Spots of blood showed up on it when she dapped her lips. She tried to hide it from me, but I noticed. The lining of her throat was compromised.

So, it wasn't *that* simple. I stared down at her decrepit body and realized that she wouldn't be able to handle space flight. She'd never make it to a core planet alive without constant attention and a rigorous schedule, but I could.

"Desmond?" she said. After her latest spell of coughing she was grimacing in pain just from talking.

I looked up from her to see a sedative sitting attentively on the table beside her bed. It was already in a syringe. All I had to do was slip a tiny bit of it into her IV and she'd fall fast asleep.

"Alora, do you trust me?" I asked.

"Of course, I do. Desmond, what's wrong with you?"

The seeds of a plan to save my people were forming in my brain, but I didn't want my decision on her conscience. She'd never accept what I was thinking about doing. "Just close your eyes," I said softly.

She gave me the look every wife gave their husband when they knew he was about to do something stupid. I didn't back down, and eventually she closed her eyes. As soon as she did, I snatched the syringe and sent what it contained streaming into her bloodstream.

"What are you..." she mouthed, her already weak voice slipping away.

I hushed her and laid her head down on her pillow. I lifted her torso, which was light as a child's, and made sure she was comfortable. Lastly, I pulled her blanket up to her neck. I couldn't imagine how cold she was with so little left of her.

"I know I don't say it enough, but you're still so beautiful," I said to her.

I knew what I had to do, but that didn't stop my hands from trembling as I reached up. I wrapped each of my index fingers around the latches of my helmet and pulled. There was a gentle hiss as the seal broke and it popped off. I dropped it to the ground and leaned over her.

The air smelled foul, but I didn't care. It'd been too long since I got to see her without a screen of glass in the way. I yanked off my gloves next and ran my exposed fingers through her knotted hair. I'd forgotten how soft it was. She was completely unconscious and the sound of her breathing was more soothing than a Velaren orchestra.

"I'll make them listen," I whispered. "I'll make them see that nobody deserves to live like this. You've fought for too long. It's my turn now."

I pulled her head towards mine and kissed her. Her lips were cold as ice. I knew I shouldn't linger since Resa might've figured out what I'd done by then, but I held her there for as long as I could, hoping that the plague would find its way to me. I never wanted to let go.

"Desmond, what are you doing!" Resa shouted from behind me, as expected. Her voice crackled with panic. "You're exposed!"

I let Alora's head fall safely back into her pillow and looked up. Resa had two others at her side; two bulky Krell nurses. It was apparently her own version of an improvised security team she'd scrapped together after she'd learned what I'd done.

"I'm sorry," I said.

The two Krell came barreling toward me but I charged right through the center of them, knocking Resa over as I burst through. I ran down the hall as fast as I could. She must've tripped the alarm because it started wailing and red lights flashed.

I looked for door tags that I recognized from earlier in order to find my way through the dizzying complex of death and despair. I could hear the footsteps of Resa and the others chasing after me between every deafening ring of the alarm.

Another nurse was waiting for me when I finally found the decontamination chamber. He went to grab me, but I ducked out of the way and threw him against the wall so hard that he was knocked unconscious. The exit was sealed for emergency protocol. I grabbed the hovering gurney next to the incapacitated nurse and rammed it into the glass door.

It didn't break.

I glanced nervously over my shoulder. Resa was catching up. I brought the gurney back as far as I could to build up speed then rammed it forward with years of grief driving my hands. The glass shattered as if a hail of bullets had been fired into it, and I leapt through.

Every person in the waiting room was on their feet when I emerged. They gasped and ducked beyond their seats as soon as they saw I was helmetless. The main lift was letting out a crowd of visitors, but that wasn't an option. It could be halted from the outside. I went to the emergency stairs instead. My tired, old legs nearly gave out during the twenty-story climb, but somehow, I made it.

Hover-car lights were blinking overhead when I emerged. People must've thought I'd finally snapped and gone mad from everything. The entire Purgat volunteer hazard squad was on their way to catch me. I knew the walkways well enough to stay out of sight and I also knew precisely where I was headed. Braxx was heading to New Terra in minutes to deliver a shipment, and I planned to join him.

His shipyard was on the edge of the city and it wouldn't take the hazard squad long to figure out I was there since everyone knew he and I were close, but I didn't need long.

I raced down a back alley and through a cluster of open shops which had barely anything left to sell. A hover-car raced by and I dove behind a counter. The cashier ran away screaming. When I got back up, my heart was racing, but I stayed poised enough to realize I should grab a few ration bars from a shelf for the trip. Then I took off. Everyone I passed from there fled even if they didn't know what was going on. We weren't stupid, after all. Any sort of ruckus in Purgat only went on because of the plague.

I ducked behind a building overlooking the shipyard as a hover-car zipped by. Once it was gone, I sprinted across a narrow street. I had to hop down a stack of crates to get down into the shipyard from the back. They were all empty. Everything being shipped out to New Terra was already loaded up, and judging by the sun, I was just in time.

Braxx was standing by the ramp of his freighter in the center of the large plot of dirt. It looked like a big, chunky pelican, if a child had drawn it, that is. The metal plating was worn and discolored, but it was the most valuable thing Tenaris Corp had left behind. Our loving benefactor's fading logo could still be read on the broad side of the hull—two hands, locked as if in eternal union.

Braxx was just finishing up counting the crates within the cargo hold. Say what you will about his business skills, but he was always diligent. I opened my mouth to shout out to him, but as I did his long, reptilian head turned toward me. Same as with Alora, I couldn't say goodbye. I couldn't involve him. I stayed quiet and crouched behind a crate. There may have been no security on Rusina, but New Terra would be crawling with guards happy to incriminate a Krell for contaminating their world.

He stared in my direction for a short while, then shrugged his big shoulders and sauntered over to the freighter's cockpit, his long tail slithering across the dirt. He pulled himself up into it, and as soon as he was in, I ran as fast as I could for the cargo hold. I was able to leap in just before it sealed shut.

I panted as I took a seat on top of a container. Once I was able to gather my breath, I stared out through the small viewport at the red lights flashing throughout the city. They would search for me for days, as if it made any difference. Purgat was already infected. It had been long before I busted out of quarantine and it would remain so long after I was gone. Unless *I* could do something about it…

~*~

It was easy when the freighter was taking off. I was going to save my wife and my people, and nobody was going to stop me. But after two weeks of seeing nothing but star-trails I began to realize the truth. There was life on almost all of them. I was just one man from one lonely world in a universe of problems.

For the first time in too long, when I thought about Alora, I didn't picture her how she was before the outbreak, when she was fulsome and gorgeous. I pictured her as she was now, fighting for every breath. Nobody deserved to live that way. Not her, not me, not even my worst enemies and their infernal, automatic-non-response. Yet there I was, threatening to cripple an entire civilization just because I wasn't ready to let the image of my beautiful wife go.

When I left Rusina, I didn't think there was any doubt the Republic's best minds could discover a cure. As I began experiencing the disease myself, wrenched over in a cramped cargo hold, begging the vomit to stay down, I wasn't so sure. How many lives would this horrible disease take before they found a cure? What if they never found one? Those were the thoughts populating my mind and getting louder.

The exit ramp controls again winked at me.

One button and it'd all be over. I rummaged through my pocket and pulled out my hand terminal. There was a picture of Alora and me when we first moved into our apartment on Rusina on the screen. We hadn't smiled like that ever again. I lifted my shaking hands to begin typing a message to her, but I stopped before getting even the first word down and dropped the device.

It was better this way. Alora would think I lost it and ran away. It was close enough to what she'd wanted. I'd rather her die thinking I was a good man than knowing the truth. That because I didn't want to lose her, I'd risked the lives of countless others.

I reached out for the exit ramp controls, and I had to pull my body closer because I was so weak from hunger. I breathed in deep. My throat was so dry that it sounded like there was a rusty grate obstructing it. I ran my fingers over the controls and let them hover over the button which would unseal the airlock. *It's the right thing to do,* I told myself.

I closed my eyes and pushed down.

Instead of a sudden whoosh and me being ripped out by a change in pressure, a whining sound rang out and an error message flashed across the controls: *The airlock cannot be released while the freighter is in motion without the specific override codes of the captain.*

I released a mouthful of air and lay back, half-chuckling and half-crying until the coughing took over. Braxx was just on the other side of a metal wall, probably thinking the error in the cargo hold was just due to the age of his ship. He may as well have been across the universe.

There was no escape. The Terra Republic was going to get *my* response and I'd have to live, or die, with the consequences. Alora—my beloved Alora—might resent me forever, but at least she might live.

~*~

Mara
Bob Williams

~*~

ZETA QUADRANT
OBLIAMOV SECTOR
HOUSE: ISHKODA

I

MARA WAS FUCKED, and she knew it. She had a good plan, cultivated in that special place in her mind like the mold that grew on the shit in the bucket in the corner of her room.

That special place in her mind reserved for crazy-ass ideas had been pivotal to her survival over the years.

She stood and paced. Her hand traced the scar that encircled her neck like the rings of Saturn.

Popan, I may die today but I'm taking you with me. And your soul won't even sniff the boundary of the Millennium Rift. No, when you die by my hands, your soul—if you even have one—will suffer a slow, torturous burn over the cinders of the Red Nova. You will suffer for what you've done. Not only to me but countless others.

II

MARA'S FIRST STRIKE was being born into House Togahn. The Togahn house existed and that was literally it. Togahn had next to no credit or monetary standing and, therefore, had no bearing on the immediate community or its partnerships.

Strike two for Mara was the location of House Togahn, in the Tera Quadrant. Long considered the bane of Quadrant Cooperative space, Tera Quadrant was where the degenerates of the Q.C. went to fester. Not only was Mara a member of the shittiest house in the quadrant, she also resided in the shittiest house within the shittiest quadrant.

For Mara, strike three came at the age of eight. Trigant Togahn, her father and master of House Togahn, sold Mara to a service interest for a much lesser value than expected and never thought of her again. He had no concept of or care for the horrors she would endure over the next fourteen years.

III

MARA'S FIRST FULL YEAR in the service interest was without question the worst year of her young life. She caught herself occasionally thinking fondly of Togahn House. *It wasn't really that bad.* The random beatings and the half-full plates of food in Togahn House became daily beatings and periodic days without food in the service interest.

The interest she labored for required her to dress in Learning Institution garb with other girls aged eight to twelve and to dance for older men who liked that sort of thing. The men weren't supposed to touch the girls, but they did. The girls weren't supposed to be left alone with the consumers, but they were.

One morning, after going more than twenty-four hours without food, her handler shook her awake and told her to report to a regular customer. Weak with fatigue and hunger—her regular schedule to dance was still maintained regardless of whether she ate or not—she could barely rise to put on her uniform. Furious, she seethed as the handler guided her to a private room where the client awaited. She was buoyed in a pit of self-loathing solely by the hatred she felt for the man sitting in front of her: Popan Doa Ishkoda.

Nine years old. No child should think of such things at nine years of age, but Mara did.

I am going to kill this man.

The door to the private room opened and a large hand firmly gripped the back of Mara's neck threw her in then slammed the door.

"Mara," Popan said. "My favorite. Come. Dance for me."

Mara couldn't move. She was nauseated and weak from starving and still saw violet star patterns from being so callously shoved in to the room.

"Mara," said Ishkoda. "I said dance." He wasted no energy feigning kindness. In this room, he could be himself: a sick, twisted predator who would be safe as long as he paid the stentz, and his favorite dish would always be served.

Mara stood transfixed. She stared at Ishkoda sitting in the large leather-clad booth, a drink in his hand and his feet on the small table in front. She tried to make her feet move. To just take the first step. *If I can't start dancing—anything—he may kill me before I get the chance to kill him.*

Mara was stunned out of her internal dialogue by a piece of ice that struck her under her right eye. The shock of how much it hurt provided her the spark she needed to begin.

"Apologies, Master Ishkoda. I am not feeling well. I am ready to begin. Apologies."

"Shut up and dance already. Do not make me regret that I asked for you by name."

Once Mara began to sway from side to side and actually started dancing, music emerged from the sound system in the walls. Despite having to deal with truly despicable people, both humanoid and Arc-Species, Mara enjoyed dancing. She was most often able to create a scenario in her head that enabled her to endure the reality of her situation and carry her through to the end of each session. Until the touching started.

Usually, as she swayed and dipped around the room, gradually getting closer, Mara imagined that a gallant and handsome space pirate would suddenly crash through the door, draw his blaster, and gun down whichever pervert was in front of her. Then he would come to her, offer his hand, and take her away from all this. And for the first time in her life nothing would be asked of her. She could just…live.

She came out of her fantasy to find herself dancing directly in front of Popan. Rage filled the empty spaces her daydream had left behind. Adrenaline kicked in; all the weakness and constraints melted away.

It's now or never.

Mara smiled coyly at Ishkoda and stuck out her hand, motioning with a finger for him to come forward. She pointed towards the floor with her open hands as if to tell him it was his turn.

He smiled and rose. He was a bit wobbly from his drink but wasted no time getting into the flow of things with Mara.

I hate you, she thought. With his legs spread wide with drunken delirium, Mara screamed and kicked him as hard as she could between the legs. He went down like a twelve-stentz credit bar.

Mara pounced on him ferociously and tried to choke him with all the force a nine-year-old girl could muster. Which, unfortunately, mattered little to a grown man. Especially a drunk, hurt, and very angry man.

Popan Doa Ishkoda struck Mara with the full force of his closed fist almost exactly where he had moments earlier with the piece of ice. The vicious blow should've killer her, but it didn't. It did knock her to the ground, delirious.

Ishkoda violently kicked her, then removed his traditional silk House Ishkoda belt and tied it around Mara's neck.

He wrapped all but a scant amount of the remaining slack around his fist and dragged her back to the open booth in the middle of the room where he lifted her up, both hands firmly around her neck.

"Do you know who I am? You would actually try to hurt me? This face is a beacon of hope throughout the Zeta quadrant and beyond!" He tossed Mara over the backside of the booth, where her feet could just touch the floor. She scrambled for footing, but found none. He was pulling her up with the belt.

As she fought desperately for her final breaths, Mara thought one last time of the handsome pirate destined to save her life…who never arrived.

IV

SOME MIGHT CALL it *loka* that the traditional silk belt Popan had used in his attempt to strangle Mara to death had broken before she died, but not Mara.

Death would have been too convenient. It would have been the blessing she deserved. It was, though she had not realized at the time, what she wanted. She'd relived that moment countless times over the last thirteen years. She was too young and stupid to understand she never stood a chance against the older man, drunk or not. Perhaps, she told herself a million times, had she not struggled but just…let go… she may have died before the belt snapped. In the end, she became damaged goods. She could dance, yes, but the scar from the friction burns around her neck made her undesirable, and the damage to her larynx had left her mute.

The service interest demanded payment from Popan for the damage to their property. In the end, Ishkoda bought her from the *SI* after a halfhearted negotiation. Ishkoda spirited her away from the grounds of the service interest, brought her to his home, and had a private cell constructed for her in a section of the oversized home no one would ever venture to.

For over a dozen years, Mara had resided in the wasteland of her own mind. She was the only one who could hear herself. She was her own best friend and her worst enemy. It was her inner voice that convinced her she wasn't going to take it anymore. That she had to get out or die trying. And it was her voice as well that would whisper, *What's the use? You wouldn't know what to do out there even if you did get escape.* Not only was Mara a brutalized captive to House Ishkoda, she was a prisoner to herself. But she was about to break free.

V

MARA'S CELL HAD no windows. No connection to the outside world in any way. A small vent installed in the ceiling kept the room temperature just above bearable.

Without the ability to see the suns rise and set, Mara completely lost track of time. She knew how many years she spent in captivity only because Popan held a despicable anniversary celebration for each completed year. Thirteen years. Mara was twenty-two years old. Every year, he reminder her she "wasn't even his type." It was the cruel candle on the cake of these despicable anniversaries. She was way too old for his tastes. No, he kept her incarcerated—repeatedly raped and molested her—simply because he could.

VI

EVERY THIRTY DAYS, Popan sent a woman into Mara's room to groom and bathe her. Grooming included a basic haircut, a trimming of the nails, and a cleanse-spray and wipe down.

Mara had not had a proper bath since her imprisonment.

Never one to waste an opportunity to be cruel, over the years, Popan had his assistant shave her head, remove her nails completely, or perform her bath with a wire brush on occasion. Just another cruel aspect of her horrid confinement.

Mara was never allowed to feel truly clean.

The timing of these grooming visits had no bearing on whether Popan was in the raping mood. Popan visited Mara in any number stages of personal hygiene and it never affected him one way or the other. He was always prepared to humiliate and degrade her regardless of how she looked or smelled.

Of all the schemes and possible ways Mara had envisioned sending Popan to burn in the Red Nova, it was the matter of a simple nail trim that finally opened her eyes to the end of her captivity.

VII

POPAN MENTIONED to Mara as he left the room the last time he violated her that he would be leaving. He had not been to Tera Quadrant in over two years and was due a tour of the educational institutions. When he wasn't raping Mara or molesting other children, he did his best to improve the Z-Quad education programs. He had to keep up appearances.

He did not give her an exact date of return but did say it wouldn't be anytime soon. "I hope nobody forgets about you down here," he said.

Mara counted on it.

While Popan was gone, a period of time which should have included two grooming cycles, Mara was visited only once. In that one visit, she was able to adequately engage the caretaker enough—despite the fact that she couldn't speak—so that her nail trim was forgotten. This was quite surprising to Mara as she used her hands to communicate.

Perfect.

VIII

MARA SAT ON THE COLD stone slab of a bed for over half of her life. She envisioned her freedom with serious clarity for the first time in years. She smiled.

She stank. She'd had only one grooming visit in…how long? *It doesn't matter.* The shit bucket was completely full. *I smell nothing but freedom.* She had no concept of the Zeta Quadrant in its current form. She had not been outside in nearly fourteen years. *I'll figure it out.* She smiled again.

She sharpened the edge of the slightly overgrown fingernail on the middle finger of her right hand back and forth over the course stone slab, her index finger already prepared. She gave herself a little test cut on her hip three days ago.

The middle finger didn't have much further to go. The idea came to her after she was given a rather hasty and seriously poor nail trim. She went to wipe something from her eye and actually opened a cut right below it from her fingernail. That a weapon existed on her person all these years had never occurred to her.

IX

"The Boga Mahn returns!" said Ishkoda as he stepped into the room. He didn't even recognize the putrid stench that would drop a normal citizen to their knees.

Fear and tension ripped through Mara as she slid her hand behind her back before Popan saw it. She fought the urge to shudder and quickly assessed the situation. In all of the scenarios she laid out in her mind, she was always lying in wait. Now, she was scrambling to remain calm. Frozen, like any other visit from Popan.

Master Ishkoda, Mara signed. *It is good to see you have returned safely. Could you send an aid to remove the excrement and schedule a grooming vis—*

Popan had continued across the room as she 'spoke' then slapped her with the full force of his momentum.

Mara stumbled backward, feeling the brutal sting of the strike as her head crunched against the wall. Her vision blurred. Tears welled in her eyes, matching the fear in her heart.

"You dare make demands of me!" roared Popan. He lunged towards her, his fist leveled to deliver the next viscous blow.

Mara blinked rapidly, not having the time to physically wipe away the tears. She made out Popan's fist swinging down in a hammer motion and thrust her arms up in an

"X" to block the strike, feeling every ounce of the hatred from the blow.

"You ungrateful bitch." Popan turned his back and walked away, shaking his head in disgust. "You…ungrateful little Tera Quad waste. If not for me you would be dead." He turned back to face her and approached for another round.

Mara's vision cleared. She saw the pure rage in his eyes.

He closed in on her once again. With her back against the wall, she had nowhere to go. She couldn't sustain another blow like the ones before. She wouldn't be able to defend herself, much less cause any damage to him.

Popan raised both his fists and stood tall over Mara. "Do you—"

Mara stood up on the hard cot beneath her, bringing here to eye-level with her tormentor, and thrust her razor-sharp finger directly into his throat.

Popan's eyes went wide with shock and fear. He was paralyzed.

Mara cocked her head slightly to the side as the warm blood leaked out.

He dropped to his knees, and Mara lowered herself with him. She couldn't speak with words, so she made damn sure she communicated with her eyes.

Popan still struggled to get away, but she hooked her fingers around his larynx.

Mara firmly placed her free hand on the back of his head and waited.

Their eyes met.

Mara took the fingers that were still inside his throat and twisted them back and forth. She watched with delight as Popan writhed in agony. She slipped her fingers loose from his throat with a final surprising ease.

With her fingers no longer staunching the flow of blood, his wound coated her with arterial spray. As his strength waned more and more, he sank back onto the filthy floor of her prison. She continued to glare into his eyes. No matter where he looked, she tracked him.

She not only wanted to see his life force snuffed out, she wanted to feel it. When he was too weak to fight her off, Mara used the nail of her index finger to continue slicing open the neck of Popan Ishkoda. She listened as he gargled and fought for his life as each breath became harder and harder to achieve.

When she felt her cut was sufficient, she eased her hand under the skin of his throat and cupped it around inside his neck. There was an immense amount of gore and blood as she wrestled through the skin, veins, and arteries. She squeezed with all the rage, pain, and suffering of the last fourteen years...and she smiled.

The Red Nova calls, you son of a bitch! You have no concept of the suffering you will endure for the rest of eternity. A slow burn on the cinders of misery awaits you for what you have done. Not just to me. For all of your victims.

X

MARA CAME TO. She was afraid to move. She noticed the cold, sticky flesh that engulfed her hand under the skin of Popan's throat. She had no idea how long she had been—what—entranced. She cautiously removed her hand from the lifeless body of her tormentor.

How long was I out?

The muscles in her legs ignited with fire when she stretched them out from under her bottom. The unforgiving cement beneath her had scrubbed her knees raw. She inspected her body as well possible without the use of a mirror. Her blood-soaked hair was matted and encrusted, with a large portion stuck solidly to her sticky and blood-drenched face.

She struggled to stand as her legs continued to scream along with the rest of her body. She'd survived the final violent confrontation. A fight for her life. Her forearm, already swollen from the traumatic blow she took, had already started to bruise.

She didn't care. Regardless of what happened next, she was free.

Mara stumbled and almost fell as she took her first free steps, her mind furiously sending messages to her legs and feet. *Get your shit together.* Mara wasn't sure how much time had passed since her battle with Popan ended, but she was surprised that no one had rushed to the room to beat or kill her. She was positive, however this ended, it would not be in the custody of a Sec-Force carrier. She would surely be killed.

She didn't know how much time she had. She still limped, fighting a new battle with her own body as she crept to the door of the cell. She took a deep breath, put her hand on the lever, and turned.

Locked!!

She turned and hobbled back to the lifeless body of Popan Doa Ishkoda. She rifled through his pants pockets with no luck.

No!

She progressed to his shirt pocket, then to his inside jacket pocket. Therein, she found a thin piece of plastic two inches wide by three inches long.

Thank the Rift!

She took the key into her sticky, blood-soaked hand and headed back for the door, her body fully tuned in and awake. Her mind was clear. Time was of the essence but she took just a moment to take it in.

Mara—the forgotten child, the captive soul, the voiceless victim—stood on the precipice of a new life.

A new beginning.

She brought the key to her lips and kissed it, then slowly waved it in front of the lever. It clicked to life and opened outward so that a sliver of light crept into the room. She pushed the door all the way open and stepped out into a long cool hallway, at the end of which was light shining through a small window in the middle of a door.

Freedom.

She turned to face the outer door. Her eyes filled with tears. Mara choked back sobs as she took the first step. Then another. As her body acclimated to this new activity, she picked up the pace. A quarter of the way down the hall, she was at a full sprint, the key held firmly in her hand.

She reached the door and looked out through the window at the beautiful Zeta Quadrant sky. She waved the key across the lever and again it responded, opening outward just a sliver. Enough so Mara was able to feel a natural breeze.

She pushed open the door and stepped out. Mara took her first full breath of fresh air.

Then she ran.

~*~

The Off-World Kick Murder Squad IV
Daniel Arthur Smith

~*~

THE RIVER CUT DEEP into the belly of the valley, bending and reversing several times as the waters crashed against boulders and escarpments. Rhia and Rhoe, as light and limber as they were, had little trouble hurling each other up into the thick limbs that thrust out over the higher banks. Hodge and I were less elegant. We leveraged our augments depending on which vines would bear us and pulled, pushed, and tossed each other when needed.

The jungle wild eventually opened to where the rushing water met a towering wall with a crown of scarlet beacons at its top—the Korean Syndicate compound.

Hodge and I, with Rhia and Rhoe on either side of us, stood in a line against the face of the wall. I pointed the barrel of my grapple up between two of the lights. The others did the same. My augments painted a grid across the heights then designated a target in the protruding ledge. I faintly chin chipped, *"All clear,"* signaling the rapid release of four compressions—*pfft, pfft, pfft, pfft*. Four clinks high above followed. We pulled our cables taut, fastened them to our waists, swung away, then planted our feet on the wall with blasters aimed at the sky. On my mark, the four of us engaged the recoils and began the four-story hike upward. The screeches and cries of nocturnal jungle creatures grew louder as we ascended above the tree line, covering what little sound we made.

A meter from the top, we stopped. Hodge and I reached to our sides to each take one of the twins' heels in hand. With a thrust from us, Rhia and Rhoe swung out and up. In a single motion, they clasped the edge of the parapet with their finger tips and pulled themselves up onto it. When they chin chipped the soft, *"Tsk, tsk,"* Hodge and I joined them.

From our perch, we surveyed the interior. Our augments overlaid the compound's geodesic sphere, the buildings with the three-dimensional translucent green images Anson had projected above the Jentu's holo-table, and from the interior of what he designated as structure three, a glowing red dot. As I scanned the buildings, numeric counters in the corner of my eye raced up and down, some calibrating to distance, others calculating possible incursion routes and the probability of success in reaching my target unseen.

"What about those two?" asked Hodge. He gestured toward two armed sentries patrolling the interior of the wall to our left.

"They haven't noticed us," I replied.

The scarlet circles surrounding their faces depicted them as low-risk, so I wasn't concerned.

"But the point is that they shouldn't be there," said Hodge.

"He's right," added Rhia. *"The residents of the compound are the only human inhabitants of a hidden planet."*

"Yeah," said Hodge. *"Not much sense to having a patrol around a lone outpost."*

I shrugged it off. *"They're most likely stretching their legs,"* I said.

"And the guns?" asked Hodge.

"You've seen the things flying around out here. I wouldn't go anywhere without a blaster."

Hodge scrunched his forehead then nodded.

"All right then," I said, sure he was on board. *"Let's drop after they pass and follow the plan. We cut between structures one and two, hug the shrubs around the fountain, and infiltrate structure three."* Everyone nodded in agreement.

When the residents cleared the area, we let loose our cables and dropped to the yard below.

The interior of the compound was lit with small LEDs lining the walk and flood lights mounted above. Had we not come from outside the wall, there'd be no telling that we were in the midst of a canopied jungle.

Rhia and Rhoe took point, tagging each other forward as Hodge and I followed. We tucked behind the meter-high bushes lining the buildings, wasting no time moving toward our target, avoiding the windows, banking that there wouldn't be any manual observation post. Security systems for outposts like this one were rarely set with a high sensitivity, but if someone was up watching monitors, alarms would go off.

When we reached the fountain between the four buildings, Rhia signaled us to stop. With a rapid hand motion, she let us know that the two sentries were crossing the side. Apparently, they had stopped. Rhia threw her hand to her ear, so I clenched my jaw to tune to their conversation.

"He pulled back," said the first, "and let it loose."

"Just like that?" asked the second.

"Just like that."

"You lucky bastard."

"What can I say? Right time, right place."

Rhia signaled that they were moving again. Whatever they were discussing didn't concern us. Then, with a wave, she signaled us forward and Rhoe passed her to take point. We followed, skirting the fountain, to the door of structure three.

The door was glass and didn't appear to have any security features other than a single buttoned pad to the side. Rhoe tapped her wrist and slid the tip of her index finger onto the glass. A window appeared in the lower right corner of my vision, an image of the inner hall, lit and empty. I nodded to Hodge and tapped the button. The door slid open, and, after a brief second, Hodge stepped through, with his long rifle Lucinda in full presentation.

The hall remained empty.

Hodge spun around to cover our tail as the three of us entered.

Small obsidian discs mounted above the doors—cameras—gave no indication as to whether they were on or recording.

We went straight for the stairwell.

"I don't like this," Hodge chin chipped.

"What's not to like?" I asked him. *"We're in the clear."*

"That's what I don't like," he said, waving Lucinda's barrel side to side as he backed up the stairs. *"Where is everybody?"*

"Asleep maybe?"

Hodge gurgled a grunt through his chin chip.

We reached the third floor without travail and gathered near the door. Rhia peeked through the square window, shrugged, pulled the door open, and entered the corridor. We followed her, the red dot in my augments bright beyond two steel doors.

Rhoe ran her hand along the seams of the door, adhered two charges—one near the top, another near the bottom—then joined Rhia and I behind Hodge.

He pointed Lucinda in the direction of the door. "Okay," he said aloud. Rhoe reached for the ignition on her wrist.

"Hold on," interrupted Hodge. He loosened his shoulders then repositioned Lucinda. "Okay. Now I'm ready," he said.

Rhoe tapped the console on her wrist—*fsst, fsst*—the charges fell away and the steel door slid apart.

If there was any type of detection system, it wasn't engaged. Our augments would have picked up lasers or weight scales. Even something as subtle as a temperature reader would've lit up in our vision. But there was nothing. The open doors revealed an empty corridor walled in by glass on either side, and at the end, another set of steel security doors.

To the left, Cerulean Blue was still hidden.

Hodge rested Lucinda's barrel on his shoulder and strolled beyond the doors.

"Nine planes," he said.

"What is it?" I asked.

"Exactly," said Hodge. He pointed to the glass wall.

I passed through the doors and there, behind the glass, bound to a chair with wide metal bands was Cerulean Blue.

"It's true then," I said.

"What's that?" asked Hodge.

It was Rhia who answered. "For years I'd heard rumors. I couldn't believe it."

But there he was, our forefather, a blue-eyed, green-scaled creature—in the shape of a man.

~*~

ABOUT THE AUTHORS

Eamon Ambrose hails from Limerick, Ireland where he lives in the West Limerick countryside with his family and an assortment of wayward animals. A self-confessed geek, and lover of all things sci-fi, Eamon decided to try his hand at writing after many years of book reviewing for various websites, as well as his own blog.

His debut, **Zero Hour: A Short Story** was an Amazon bestseller, and became so popular it was continued as a serial, and is now collected in a single novel. As well as writing for several upcoming anthologies, Eamon regularly blogs about his experiences in publishing and still reviews books when he finds the time, as well as working on his next project, a modern fantasy novel.

For more information, visit eamonambrose.com

Jessica West (a.k.a. West1Jess) is currently pursuing a state of self-induced psychosis, also known as writing. In the past, she has worked for Wal-Mart, a lawyer, and a bank. Now if she could just get a couple years experience with the IRS and the NSA, world domination is in the bag.

Jess lives in Acadiana with three daughters still young enough to think she's cool and a husband who knows better but likes her anyway.

For more information, visit west1jess.com

Rhett C. Bruno has been writing since before he can remember, scribbling down what he thought were epic stories when he was young to show to his friends and family. He currently works at an Architecture firm, but that hasn't stopped him from recording the tales bouncing around inside of his head.

Rhett is the bestselling author of *The Circuit Trilogy*, *Titanborn*, and *From Ice to Ashes*. Please subscribe to his newsletter for exclusive access to updates about his work and the opportunity to receive limited content and ARCs. For a limited time, you'll also receive a FREE digital copy of Book one in *The Circuit Trilogy-The Circuit: Executor Rising*.

For more information, visit rhettbruno.com

Bob Williams currently lives in Nashville, Tennessee after stops in Mississippi, Louisiana, Ohio, and Washington. He lives with his beautiful 6 year old daughter Kate, dogs Hank Henry, and two cats Cassidy and Wally. Bob sincerely hopes you enjoy reading his words as much as he enjoys writing them.

Daniel Arthur Smith is a USA Today bestselling author. His titles include *Spectral Shift*, *Hugh Howey Lives*, *The Cathari Treasure, The Somali Deception*, and a few other novels and short stories. He also curates the phenomenal short fiction series *Tales from the Canyons of the Damned*.

He was raised in Michigan and graduated from Western Michigan University where he studied philosophy, with focus on cognitive science, meta-physics, and comparative religion. He began his career as a bartender, barista, poetry house proprietor, teacher, and then became a technologist and futurist for the Fortune 100 across the Americas and Europe.

Daniel has traveled to over 300 cities in 22 countries, residing in Los Angeles, Kalamazoo, Prague, Crete, and now writes in Manhattan where he lives with his wife and young sons.

For more information, visit danielarthursmith.com

~*~

www.ingramcontent.com/pod-product-compliance
Lightning Source LLC
Chambersburg PA
CBHW020312150626
46552CB00022B/2845